P9-CPV-682

The
Broken
Bike Boy
and the
Queen
of 33rd
Street

SHARON G. FLAKE

illustrations by
FRANK MORRISON

JUMP AT THE SUN BOOKS

NEW YORK

Text copyright © 2007 by Sharon G. Flake
Illustrations copyright © 2009 by Frank Morrison

Printed in the United States of America
First Disney•Jump at the Sun paperback edition, 2009
3 5 7 9 10 8 6 4 2
This book is set in 12.5-point Hightower.
Library of Congress Cataloging-in-Publication Data on file.
ISBN 978-1-4231-0035-5
ILS J689-1817-1 10361
Visit www.hyperionbooksforchildren.com and
www.sharongflake.com

To All the
Queens,
Kings,
And Princely Gents
Of North Philadelphia:
Dream On,
For the Universe Is Yours
If Only You Believe

For Symone Granville
A girl
A star
A gem
Up
Far
A million twinkling lights
are yours to read by at night
Grab a cloud
Read out loud
For angels know a good story
when they hear one.

CHAPTER 1

I AM A QUEEN. I live in a castle, right across the street from the John Howard housing project. Every day right after school, I run to my bedroom window and open it wide—even in the middle of winter when the wind blows wet snow up my nose. I watch for my knight in shining armor. He's ten years old, in the fifth grade like me, and rides a bike—a two-wheeler with rusty spokes and a busted seat.

My friend Symone says that knights lived a long time ago and rode horses, not broken bikes with patched tires. But I think knights are still around today. I know for sure they are, because I know something that Symone doesn't know; that nobody knows about the broken bike boy.

You see, I was someplace I wasn't supposed to be. And a fire-breathing dragon started chasing after me. She had a tongue as long as a river and slimy fingers that ruined everything they touched. And right when I figured I was done for, my knight in shining armor rode up on that broken bike and, well, I think I will tell you the whole story right from the beginning.

You see, the first day I met him, it was a Tuesday, my most terrible day of the week. I remember the day because I was having a very nice dream, then Mother walks into my room, waking me up.

"Queen. Queen!" Mother says, pulling covers off my head.

I love to sleep, so I don't like people waking me. "Go away."

I don't like listening to my mother, only my father. Mother thinks I'm spoiled. So when he comes into the room, rubs my back, and whispers my name, "Queen. Time for school," I get up smiling.

I hold my arms out so Father can give me my morning hug.

"You make it so hard," he tells Mother. "But it's as easy as pie to get the girl moving. See?" he says, carrying me to the bathroom and standing me on a thick, purple towel he puts on the floor just for me. "You are a queen," he says, bowing. "Queen of . . ."

"Queen of Thirty-third Street," I say, taking my purple toothbrush and touching him on each shoulder like real queens do with their scepters. "You may go now," I say, turning on the hot water spigot.

"Shall we wait breakfast for you, milady?" Father asks.

"Yes. Tea with milk, and lemon sugar cookies, please."

Father walks out the bathroom backward, because real queens never want to see a servant's behind parts.

Mother is in the living room, saying what she always says. "You're ruining her, John. She believes that queen stuff, you know."

I stand on my tiptoes and look at myself in the mirror. "She's my queen," I say, right along with Father. "And nobody'd better ever forget that."

I used to be homeschooled until two years ago. But I go to regular school now. Mother thought I needed to be around other kids. She said she didn't like how grown-up and stuck-up I was acting. Only, I can't help it if I'm cute and smarter than most kids my age.

Mother is upset. "Get out the mirror and come eat your breakfast, Queen!"

Father is always nice to me. "Baby girl, time to eat."

I put on my purple striped shirt, white socks, and black patent leather shoes and go into the kitchen. Father is the cook in our family. He makes the best eggs and ham. And even though he asks me every morning what I want for breakfast, he makes whatever he likes. And I always love it too.

After I finish eating, I wipe my mouth. "Hmmm. The queen is very pleased indeed."

"Well, Queen, might I say that there won't be any clean dishes to eat off this evening if Her Majesty doesn't empty the sink and put them in the dishwasher right now?"

Father clears his throat. That means for Mother to stop talking. Only, she doesn't care about stuff like that so she keeps running off at the mouth, telling Father that with three kids in college, money is tighter than a size-eight foot in a size-six shoe. "So I think we should cut back on spending so much money on Queen and her foolishness."

Mother is talking about my fairy tale books—I have 157 of them. And she is talking about other things that Father buys me that she doesn't approve of. Father winks and says there is always enough money in the bank to buy me what I want.

Father works two jobs. My mother works one job and babysits. They own the apartment building we live in. It's just me at home now. I'm the youngest. My brothers, Marcus, Kingston, and Joshua, are all at college. When they send me letters, they put golden crown stickers on the envelopes.

"Queen," Father says, "ready for school?"

I kiss him. And ask him to tell me again why he named me Queen. He reminds me that he gave me the name because he always wanted people to remember that I was someone extra special. I finish the story. "And one day Queen Elizabeth was on TV and you said, 'I'll name her Queen so people will look up to her and respect her too.'"

I love the story. Mother is sick of it. "John," she says, "she will be late for school."

I open the front door. "Shall we take the red car or the blue one?"

"Hmmm. Blue," Father says.

"Queen." Mother points to the dishes still in the sink and on the table then sticks out her lips. "Kisses."

I kiss her. She squeezes me tight. "You're the queen of this castle, that's for sure."

Father and I walk out the door, get in our car, and head for school. My stomach aches and I tell him that I want to stay home.

"You must see your royal subjects," he says. "They await you."

I look out the window. Father works the radio, trying to get his favorite station, so he doesn't see what I see. Kids sticking their tongues out at me. Kids putting up their fists and rolling their eyes. Kids who think I am a royal pain in the neck.

CHAPTER 2

"QUEEN MARIE ROSSEAU," the teacher says. "Sit down and zip your lips, please."

Everyone laughs. I don't think it's funny. All I said was she made a mistake and spelled *superstitious* the wrong way. "You left out a T," I told her.

Mrs. McBride doesn't like me. She thinks I am a spoiled know-it-all who makes trouble for her. I know what she thinks because I heard her say it to another teacher once. I started to tell my father. But

Mother and Father say I am a tattletale too. So I kept it to myself.

"Mrs. McBride. Mrs. McBride," I say, waving my hand in the air. "I know the answer."

She walks right by me and calls on Leslie. Then she calls on Sara, Peter, Jason, Kajune, and two other kids. The whole time my hand is in the air, she walks by me, pointing over my head to other students. Ignoring me. So I wave both my hands side to side like they do at football games.

Mrs. McBride stomps over to my desk in brown boots as pointed as spears. "Miss Rosseau. What do you want?"

I sit on my hands. "I know the answer."

Her foot taps the floor like mine does when I'm waiting to use the girls' room and kids are taking too long. "You always know the answer," she says, walking to the front of the room. "Let someone else show what they know for once, Your Royal Highness."

Mrs. McBride is pretty. She's got skin the color of caramel candy, and eyes as big as quarters. But the words that come out of her mouth are ugly sometimes. They can hurt and scratch like a pushpin left on your chair. "Well," I say, "I guess I don't have to tell you that the answer is twenty-two."

The principal interrupts our class, so Mrs. McBride doesn't have a chance to get mad at me. Our principal has a new boy with her—and he smells. As soon as he walks into the room, before we even know his name, his odor flies around the room like a witch on a broom.

"Don't sit him next to me," Elroyan says, making noises with his chair when he moves it to the side.

Markeeta whispers in my ear, only, she can't really whisper, so when she says, "He pees himself," I think he hears her way up front.

I don't know why I do it, but I whisper in Shelby's ear. "He wets the bed."

Shelby passes it on, so by the time the boy gets to his new desk in the middle of the room, someone in the back row points to him and says, "Skunk in the room. Close your nose."

Mrs. McBride tries to make us stop, but we cover our noses with both hands anyhow.

"Stop it. Right this instant!"

The boy's name is Leroy. His eyes water when

he looks around the room. But he doesn't get mad. He laughs. "I do have a skunk at home," he says. "He funks up all my clothes."

It is a fib. We all know that. But nobody says anything else until lunchtime.

Our class sits up near the front of the cafeteria, close to where the milk, juice, and cookies are sold. Every class is supposed to sit together, but Melnick Washmiller, who talks too much and eats with his mouth open, does what he wants. So he leaves the assigned table where his class sits and walks over to our table. Mrs. McBride is at another table, talking to a teacher. She sees Melnick, but she doesn't say anything to him.

Melnick asks where Leroy lives.

"I live on Thirty-third Street."

"Where?"

"On the corner. By the park."

Melnick looks at us and winks. "Which house?"

I can tell that Leroy is not like other boys in our class. He stinks like moldy clothes or feet stuck in socks that get washed once a year. His clothes are too small. And he uses words bigger than his head. "I live in the house adjacent to the park."

Melnick doesn't even know what that word means. "Huh?"

"Next to the park, knucklehead," I say.

He pushes me. "If I'm a knucklehead, then you're a, you're a . . ." He looks around the room at pictures of food on the walls. "You're a cheeseburger head with onion breath."

I push Melnick and he falls on the floor. Mrs. McBride sees what I did and makes me stand in the corner for the rest of the period. After a while, all the other kids go outside to play. It's really warm, and the windows in the cafeteria don't open, so you sweat down to your underwear when you stay inside too long.

Whenever I stand in the corner, I close my eyes and see myself sitting on a throne in a long white gown with a gigantic ruby crown on my head. I'm telling all the people who serve me to polish the silver and scrub the floors clean. Everything must be done quickly, I say, because we are going to have a royal party, the biggest party in all the land. Everyone is invited. Rich people. Poor people. Kids and parents too. We will dance and sing and eat until we're stuffed. I am queen of all the land. Queen of the world, I think to myself.

Leroy comes back inside. "Queen is a funny name."

I am used to kids saying that, so I ignore him.

He doesn't care that I'm not speaking to him. "My brother's name is Chop. People say he's got a funny name too."

I turn around. "That's a dumb name. I don't have a dumb name."

Leroy comes closer.

"You're supposed to be outside, not in here bothering me." I squeeze my nose while I talk so I don't have to smell him. I wonder if he can smell what he smells like. "Do you think that people with dogs at home know that their houses stink?"

"Huh?"

I ask the question again.

He walks over to the door. "I don't know," he says, opening it. "I don't have a dog."

I can see everyone outside jumping rope and swinging high up in the air.

"Your house stink or something?" he asks.

"We don't stink!"

"I didn't say you did. But maybe your house does."

When I get mad, the sides of my nose spread like moth wings. "I don't stink. We don't stink. You stink," I say, just when Mrs. McBride walks into the room.

She grabs hold of my arm. "Young lady, you have a long way to go before you learn to conduct yourself like a real queen." She stares down at me. "You walk around this school like you live in a castle, and—"

"I do live in a castle."

Mrs. McBride stops. She tells Leroy to go outside and play. It is just me and her in the cafeteria. She pokes the side of my head with her finger. "Your parents fill your head with fairy dust, and then I have to put up with all of your nonsense." She takes me by the arm and drags me back to our classroom.

I live in a castle. I do. If you rode up Thirty-third Street, you'd see that I was telling the truth. Our house is brick. Red brick. One side of the building is round, like a tower. There is a balcony, like the ones queens stand on in fairy tales. And the top is as pointed as a dunce cap, just the way a real castle is. I've told Mrs. McBride this. Told her that my father said it was a real castle once, long, long ago. Only, she never agrees. She just says there are no castles where I live. "No queens either," she said. I told my father that. He came in to talk to her about it and she never said it again.

When Mrs. McBride opens the door, she stops a minute and stares down at me. "If I could wash your mouth out with soap . . ."

I cover my mouth with my hands.

"I would. If I could. But I can't," she says, handing me a piece of chalk. "But I can make you write on the blackboard one hundred times, 'I will not be mean. I will not hurt other people's feelings.'"

I like to write on the board, so I don't mind. But inside my head, I am not writing what she wants at all. I am writing a letter to the people that live in the land that I am queen of. "My royal subjects," I write, "I am having a really bad day."

CHAPTER 3

I GET A RIDE TO SCHOOL. But I walk
home because my father is still at work then. I
always walk home with Symone Santiago. She is
my best friend. We go to the movies and museums
together with our moms. We never fight or pick on
each other, though. I like that. On the way home I
tell her that Leroy says my house smells.

"Has he been in your house before?"

"No."

Symone walks into the corner store to buy candy. "Then why'd he say it?"

I put a quarter on the glass counter and ask for two pieces of caramel. "Do you think it stinks?"

"Yep."

"My house does not stink!" I pick up my nickel and stuff it in my pocket. "Leroy stinks."

For a while, I walk with my head down. I don't even open up the caramel, which is my favorite.

"I guess it doesn't really stink. But sometimes it smells funny." Symone opens her cherry sucker and drops the paper on the ground. "Like, like lots and lots of vitamins. Or milk spilled on the rug that somebody forgot to clean up."

Old milk smells like vomit I tell her. "You think my house smells like vomit?"

Symone pulls the sucker out of her mouth and shows me her red tongue. "Leroy smells really bad. Your house hardly stinks at all."

I start walking faster—too fast for Symone. She says for me to slow down so she can catch up. But I want to get home and see if she and Leroy are right.

"Does our house stink?" I ask Mother when I

get in. She is on the phone. She kisses my cheek and says for me not to disturb her. I stick my nose out and sniff. I get on my hands and knees, put my nose right on the couch cushions and breathe in hard. "Symone says our house smells like old milk."

Mother puts her finger to her lips. "Shhh."

I leave my backpack on the dining room floor. I smell the air, the tablecloth, and the chairs. I go into my parents' room and sniff my mother's sweaters, my father's undershirts, and their used towels. Then I run to my room, digging in drawers and smashing used ribbons and hair scrunchies to my face. "They smell like grease, but they don't stink." I open my closet and make a face at all the dirty clothes in the basket. At first I hold my nose. After a minute, I let it go, get down on my knees, and put my nose right inside the pile. It reeks. But dirty clothes are supposed to reek. Anyhow, they don't stink so bad that you could smell 'em in the living room or way in the kitchen. "Our house does not stink!"

"What on earth?" Mother says, getting off the phone.

I tell her what Symone said. She says that Symone must have been pulling my leg. "Our house always smells fresh." She reaches for my hair and rebraids a plait. "We clean it top to toe every Saturday."

I sniff again. "Our house doesn't stink. Leroy stinks."

Mother says she doesn't know any Leroy, but she had better not hear me say that about someone else again. "It's rude." She goes into my drawer and puts a purple plaid ribbon on the end of my long, beautiful braid. "You didn't say it to his face, did you?"

"No."

"Good."

I look in the mirror and wave my hand side to side like a real queen. "If it's true, why can't you say it?"

Mother reaches for another ribbon. "Do you want people telling you everything they think is true about you?"

I look in the mirror again. I poke my belly. It jiggles. Sometimes kids say I eat too much. They moo, like cows. Or finish their lunch all except the brown crust, then turn to me and ask if I want it. "I guess we shouldn't say everything we think."

Mother kisses my forehead. "You are a little queen: a little queen with a big heart."

When the phone rings and she leaves the room, I go to my bedroom and put on the paper crown I made for myself. I walk out on the balcony and wave.

Mr. Riley, our second-floor tenant is standing on the corner across the street, ready to cross. He waves back at me. "Queen for a day," he says, smiling.

I bow to my loyal subject and look up and down the street. It's busy with people. Some are driving cabs and cars. Others are walking, playing cards, or standing on corners laughing with friends. A few are troublemakers. I am not scared of them, but Mother and Father say to watch out. They take what isn't theirs and hurt people for no reason.

"Hello, Mrs. Jefferson." I'm waving to a lady at the bus stop. She lives on the first floor of our building.

"Hey, Queen," she shouts. "How's the prettiest little girl in the world?"

I think about the carrot raisin muffins she makes me sometimes, and I start licking my lips.

That's when I see a boy ride by on a bicycle. He is standing up. The bike has a broken seat. When Mrs. Jefferson yells up to me to come get muffins later on, the boy looks up. It's Leroy, riding a broken bike. It is the first time I see him on that thing. And even though Mother says calling names is not nice, I do it anyhow. "Leroy. We don't stink. You do!"

"Queen." Mother is pulling me back from the balcony. "That is the cruelest thing I've ever heard you say."

She has on a purple polka-dotted apron and is holding a wooden spoon in her hand. "Stay right there, little boy." She looks at me and says for me to bring him up here and apologize right in front of her.

I try to explain. "He smells like feet, and pee, and yuck. Everyone says so."

She points to the door. "You *get*, young lady." She smacks her hand with the spoon. "Or else you will be in big, big trouble."

CHAPTER 4

LEROY'S BIKE IS BLUE. But mostly it is
brown rust with missing spokes. Nobody stares at
his bike, though, 'cause lots of kids around here ride
bikes like that. Not me. My bike is red and shiny
and fast. I tell Leroy that when I get downstairs.

"Can I ride it?" he asks.

"No. It's mine."

He puts his foot on the broken black pedal and
starts to take off.

"My mother wants you."

He looks up to our apartment. "Why?"

"She just does."

"For what?"

"'Cause."

"'Cause why?"

I kick his tire. "When my mother says come, you're supposed to come, not ask a bunch of ridiculous questions."

Leroy leaves his bike on the side of our house. We walk three flights to my apartment. "She got cookies?"

"We always have cookies."

He rubs his stomach. "And milk?"

I roll my eyes. "Everybody's got milk."

"And . . ."

You stink and you're greedy, I want to say. But if I do, Mother will put me on punishment, so I keep quiet. I look at his run-over shoes and his extra-small brown shirt. And the whole time we are going up the steps, I make sure not to breathe through my nose.

Mother shakes his hand. "Well, hello, young man."

Leroy smiles. "I am exceptionally pleased to meet you."

I just look at him.

"My, my," Mother says. "You have wonderful manners. Where do you live?"

He points across the street to his housing project. There are ten buildings over there, four floors each. Sometimes it is not so safe. But the people there have always been nice to me.

Mother asks if he just moved in there. Greedy Leroy asks where we keep the cookies and tells her he only likes milk that is ice cold. Mother says he may have whatever he likes, and she makes me go to the kitchen with her to make him a plate.

"See? He does smell."

"Queen!" She opens the fridge and takes out chocolate milk. "Please watch your mouth." She gets peanut-butter cookies from the white cookie jar shaped like a polar bear. Right when she has it all on a tray and is headed for the living room, she turns around and puts the tray down on the table. She opens the fridge, takes out bread, mayo, lunch meat, and cheddar cheese, and makes a gigantic sandwich.

"Where's mine?"

She never answers. She picks up the tray and leaves.

"Leroy. Let's eat," she says, like she is going to have a sandwich too.

He sits down at the table, then jumps right up. "Where's your bathroom?" He runs off to wash his hands and then sits back down. "You work?" he asks Mother, like that's his business.

Mother tells him she has a job but today is one of her days off. "I'm a nurse. I work three days a week, and I sometimes babysit on weekends."

He noses the air like a raccoon. "Oh. That's why it smells like that in here."

That makes me mad, so I just say what I'm thinking. "You funked up our house. That's why."

Mother gets angry with me. "Queen, you are never to insult a guest in our home again!"

I apologize, but only because she makes me. Leroy keeps eating. First he drinks all of his chocolate milk. Then he eats the taco chips and garlic pickles Mother put right next to his sandwich.

Mother wipes pickle juice off his chin. "You won't have room for your sandwich and cookies."

Leroy tells her he has a quadruple stomach, like a cow, so he can eat our whole house if he wants. He is right. He eats all the food and still asks for more milk, another sandwich, and cookies to take home with him.

Mother pinches his cheek. "Why don't you ride to school with Queen and her dad in the morning?"

Father would never have said anything like that. He knows that mornings are our special time together. I don't even want Symone with us then.

Leroy doesn't want to ride with us anyhow. "No thanks. I ride my bike to school."

Mother puts all of his food in a big, brown shopping bag. "Couldn't someone steal your bike while you're in school?"

I let her know that nobody wants a broken bike.

Leroy looks hurt. Mother looks angry. So I sit down and tell Leroy what Mother wants me to say, but I don't really mean it. "You may ride with us in the morning."

CHAPTER 5

"QUEEN," FATHER SAYS, sticking his head in the bathroom, "your royal coach is waiting."

I wear purple every day because Father says purple is a sign of royalty. Today I am wearing a purple dress with tights to match. My earrings are gold crowns that hang from little purple chains and dangle when I move my head.

"Is milady ready?"

"Yes, she is, Sir Father."

He puts his arm out and I take hold of it all the way to the front door. Mother reminds him that Leroy is going with us too. And she tells him again how awful I was to him yesterday.

Father pinches my cheek. "She was just having a bad day, weren't you?"

"Yes, Father."

He smiles down at me. "Because a queen is never rude on purpose, is she?"

I look over at Mother. "No, Father."

Father kisses my cheek and kisses Mother on the lips. "Then let's go get Leroy," he says, closing the door behind us.

Leroy smells different. Like pee mixed with perfume. "Hi," he says.

"Queen? Are you going to introduce me to your friend?" Father's unlocking the car door so Leroy can get in.

I point to him. "That's Leroy."

He shakes his hand. "Hello, Leroy. Welcome into our carriage." Father is just like Mother. He acts like there is nothing different about Leroy.

"Our carriage is special. It only carries royalty. Queens," he says, winking my way. "Kings," he says, patting his own shoulder. "Princes, court jesters, maiden ladies . . ."

Leroy sits up straight. "I can be a prince."

"No you can't," I tell him.

He shouts at me. "Yes I can! I can be anything I want."

I squeeze my nose closed. "A prince doesn't smell like rotten cabbage."

Father gets angry. He says the same thing as Mother. "You are never to insult a guest again, or you'll be punished."

I cross my arms and hum in my head because I don't care what Father or Mother says. I don't like Leroy, and it isn't right for them to make him ride to school with me.

For a long time nobody in the car talks. Then Leroy asks what kind of queen I am. I'm not speaking to him so I don't answer.

"I think she's a sourpuss queen today, Leroy."

"I'm an African prince," Leroy says, "from Senegal."

Father drives slow. Most times I like that

because it gives us more time together. Today, I wish he would speed up.

"Really, Leroy?"

Leroy isn't just smelly and greedy. He fibs too. He sits in our car and tells father that he's been to Senegal. "I swam in the Gambia River." He pushes his arms and hands out like he is swimming in a park pool. "It's seven hundred miles long and I swam every inch!" Leroy's fibs just get bigger. "We went a lot of places when I lived in Africa. One country had pink water. Another country had antelopes and zebras that would eat buttered popcorn right out my hands."

I cover my ears, but I still hear him talking.

"Some beaches have black sand."

I tell him that there is no such thing. Father corrects me. He's an English teacher, but sometimes they make him teach geography and history as well. He knows everything. So he tells me there are places in Africa with water and beaches just like Leroy described. "Africa is a magnificent continent, full of beauty." He turns Leroy's way. "I guess you *are* a real prince." When we get to school, he opens the car and bows to him.

"In Africa, we sometimes eat with our fingers, but here they say it's not good manners," Leroy says.

I kiss Father and try to get away from Leroy.

"Well, Prince," Father says, shaking his hand, "you must come dine with us at our house. It's not fancy like maybe your place in Africa, but . . ."

Leroy folds his arms. "I lived in a palace."

"Oh, you did not," I say.

Leroy ignores me. "It had gold floors and murals on all the walls."

I look at Father.

"A mural is a huge painting. It could cover an entire wall or the side of a building."

In my head I am counting. It's something my parents taught me to do when I think I am going to get so mad that it will get me into trouble. I am on number twenty-three when Leroy invites himself to our place for dinner tonight.

Father smiles, and I know what he is thinking, so I speak up. "No. You can't come."

Father says yes, just to upset me, I think. Leroy says he will bring pictures of his family and their palace.

When we are almost in the building, I ask Leroy how come he lives in our neighborhood if he's got a palace back home. Of course he doesn't answer. And I know why. Leroy Wright has never lived in a palace. He has never been to Senegal. And when he comes to dinner tonight, he won't have any pictures either.

CHAPTER 6

"QUEEN'S GOT A BOYFRIEND. Queen's got a boyfriend." Jessica points at me and tells everybody that she saw me get out of my father's car with Leroy.

"He's not my boyfriend!"

"Yeah he is."

Before school starts, we all have to go to the school yard to play. Jessica is with Shawn, Markeeta, Kelly, Kyle, and James. "Ain't you her boyfriend, Leroy?" she asks.

"Yep," Leroy says, kicking a soccer ball back to some kids by the fence.

I push him good. "No you're not." I kick at his leg, but he moves so I miss. "Tell 'em. You're not my boyfriend."

Everyone laughs. Shawn asks what my name would be if Leroy and me got married.

James says it real loud. "Queen Pee." Then he gets down on one knee. "Queen Pee, will you marry me?"

It's not funny. I tell them so. But they keep saying it. That's when I throw down my book bag and run after Shawn, Kyle, and James. I run through a game of hopscotch. Don't even stop when the boys playing basketball yell at me for breaking up their game. I chase them around the school yard three whole times, but I never catch up to them. When I'm done, Leroy says, "They shouldn't have said that. It's not nice to tease people."

The bell rings. I pick up my purple backpack and get in line. Leroy's following me. I cross my arms and make my meanest face. "You cannot ride to school with us ever again."

He acts like he doesn't even care. "In Africa we mostly ride bikes anyhow."

I tell him that he never lived in Africa and he isn't a prince and he'd better stop saying that he is.

Jessica's last name begins with an *S* so she is standing in line behind me, listening to every word Leroy says.

He stands up tall. "I'm a prince," he says, like she cares.

Jessica just stares at him. Then she turns her head to the side and looks at me like maybe there are flies in my hair. "You're a prince?" she asks Leroy. "A real one?"

Leroy should just be quiet. Only, he keeps talking, telling her what he told Father about being a real prince. Jessica hops up and down, turning her arms in circles like she's jumping rope. "Prince Pee and Queen Pee got married and had a baby. The baby's name was Pee-Pee."

Other kids start singing too. "Prince Pee and Queen Pee got married and had a baby . . ."

I explain that a queen marries a king, not a prince, and *they* have children. But the kids don't care. They like the song, I guess, so they sing louder. I try to get Mrs. McBride to make them stop. Only, she doesn't like me, so whenever I raise my hand she ignores it. "You tell her," I say to Leroy.

"I like the song."

Jessica claps her hands and sings even louder.

"I don't smell like pee," I say.

Leroy puts his nose on my hair and sniffs. "What you smell like then?"

I push him away. "I don't smell like anything."

He tells me he has a sister and she smells like medicine. "And I have a brother who smells like, who smells like . . ."

I put my fingers in my ears. "Liar. Liar. Liar," I say right when Mrs. McBride grabs me by my arm and snatches me out of line.

"Queen! What did you say?"

"Nothing."

"We don't use that word. You know that, right?"

My head goes up and down.

"You must like writing on the blackboard, don't you?"

"No, ma'am."

She tells the class to keep their eyes glued in front of them and follow her quietly into the building and to their seats. "And you, Queen. You head straight for the blackboard and write fifty times, 'I will not call Leroy names.'"

Everyone is supposed to be quiet while they walk. Only, while Mrs. McBride is way up front, Markeeta and Jessica make up a brand-new song. "Queen is smart. Queen is pretty. But nobody likes her except her kitty."

It doesn't make sense, because I don't have a kitty. But everyone thinks it's funny, so they sing it quietly—first two, then five, then nine kids all together. Mrs. McBride doesn't hear them, so she keeps marching. I stare down at my pretty pink shoes until they walk me into class and over to the blackboard where my favorite color chalk is.

CHAPTER 7

MRS. MCBRIDE CALLED my mother. My
mother didn't like what I had said to Leroy. She
and Father said I was getting out of hand. So they
put me on punishment. They said I couldn't visit
with Symone for two whole weeks. It wasn't fair.
Symone, me, and both our moms were supposed to
go to the movies and get our fingernails and toes
painted later. My mother canceled everything.
Symone got mad at me, like it was all my fault. "It

wasn't," I told her. "Mother does stuff like that for no reason."

Father caught me on the phone talking to Symone and he made me hang up. Later on I sneaked and called my brother Kingston. He is always nice to me. "Don't worry," he said. "Tomorrow I will put something special in the mail for you."

I know what it is. He told me, since I don't like secrets. It's a box of candy that his girlfriend picked up at a store for me, a purple ring, and a T-shirt that says Queen of the House. "Don't wear it until you're off punishment," he said. Then like always, he told me how much he loves me. Right after that I called my other brothers, to see what they would send me.

I'm standing on my balcony, watching Leroy hop on his bike and ride across the street to our place. Before he does, he rides up and down his side of the block. He is by himself, like always. But he is laughing and talking. Riding that bike like it is shiny and new—not broken, with crooked handlebars and no seat.

I look at him ride, and think of my bike. It's better than his, only I never ride it. I don't know how. Father tried teaching me a million times, only I still fall off.

Right away Leroy comes into our house fibbing, telling Father that he has seventeen brothers and sisters. He asks if he can eat sitting on the floor. "I don't use knives and forks," he says, holding up all ten fingers. "In my village, we eat our meals out of a big bowl my mother puts in the middle of the table."

Mother comes out the kitchen and kneels down beside him. She asks how long he has lived in America. He says he came when he was six years old. "You speak our language well," she says. "You don't even have an accent."

Leroy pulls off his socks and picks lint from between his toes. "I practice extremely hard. I don't want to sound different."

Father bows. "Prince Leroy," he says, "it is an honor to have you in our home again."

All of a sudden Father likes sitting on floors too. He sits down right next to Leroy. Mother says it would be nice to eat on the floor, picnic style. So she goes into the kitchen and comes back with a green tablecloth. She spreads it on the floor and puts gray plastic dishes all over it. Father pulls off his shoes and socks, and sits with his legs crossed just like Leroy. I tell Father I don't want to eat with Leroy's fuzzy feet in my face. Mother pulls off her sandals. She wiggles her toes and says it feels good to have them set free.

"Queen. Take our guest's shoes to your bedroom and sit them there, please."

I tell her no.

Father picks up his and Mother's shoes. He takes them to their bedroom. "Queen," he tells me when he comes back, "Prince Leroy is our guest. We must treat him with respect."

I shake my head no.

Leroy bends over, sniffs his feet, and smiles like he is smelling Mother's butter pecan pound cake. "I never use powder. It makes my feet itch."

Father tells me to do what he says. He means it. So I pick up those dirty sneakers by the tips of my fingers and carry them into my room. After I'm done, I wash my hands seven times.

When I come back, Leroy's talking, saying his

village was burned down by rebels. They stole all the grain and burned down mud houses with straw roofs. "Even our palace was destroyed."

Mother puts baked fish on his plate. Father puts tomatoes and cucumbers in his bowl and pours grape soda in his glass. Leroy digs his fingers in his food and eats. "We flew to London," he says, sucking his fingers. "Then we took a boat here."

"All of you?" Mother asks, sticking her fingers in her food and eating like him.

"All of us."

"My goodness. How many people came in all?"

Leroy closes one eye and sticks more food into his mouth. "Eighty."

I think about his place across the street. "Eighty people live with you over there?"

He claims only his mother lives there. The rest of his family lives in different houses in different cities. "But one day we will all be united again."

His fingers touch his toes. His head bends low and he doesn't say anything for a while. Mother wipes her hands and pats his back. She asks if there is anything she can do. He tells her no. "My brothers and sisters write to me all the time." He holds his plate out for more asparagus and dirty rice. "Sometimes I get twelve letters in the mail, all in one day."

I see Father look at Mother like maybe he doesn't believe him. I put my fork down and tell Leroy to show us his pictures. Naturally he doesn't have any. That makes him quiet again. And it makes Mother and Father even nicer to him. "Cake?" they ask. "Ice cream? More soda?"

They are treating him like somebody special. I am glad when he leaves. But as soon as the door closes, and Mother and Father watch him cross the street and go into his building, Mother comes to my room. She tucks me in and kisses me good night. Long after it is quiet in our house, I sneak out of my room. I get on the computer and type in the word "Africa." I want to know for sure—do people really eat with their fingers? Are there palaces and mud huts still today? Or is Leroy fibbing, like always?

CHAPTER 8

I LOVE BOOKS. Symone likes to watch TV. I
love to dress up in gowns that Mother wore when
she was a teenager and a college homecoming
queen. So while I am putting on makeup and dress-
ing up, Symone is watching her favorite television
show.

"Symone."

"Shhh. This is the best part."

I hold up the ends of my gown and tiptoe into

Mother's room. The bottom of her closet is full of shoes she never wears. I pick out the highest, most sparkly pair. They are greener than grass and as shiny as a paper star covered in glitter. One foot slides in nice and easy. I hold on to the wall when I put the other shoe on. I walk over to the long mirror hanging on Father's closet door. Pretty is important to me. So I'm smiling at my pretty dress and shoes, my pretty face and hair. "Mirror, mirror on the wall, who is the fairest of them all?" I say in my sweetest voice.

I can talk deep and even croak like a frog. "You are, my queen."

"Mirror, mirror on the wall, who is the smartest of them all?"

"You, my lovely one."

There are twelve mirrors in our house. There used to be nineteen. Some were given to me as presents, others I found at school. Mother thought I stared at myself too much so she got rid of the rest. But all the fairy tale books have mirrors or ponds or crystal balls that people look into so they can see themselves better.

"Mirror, mirror—"

"Queen!"

It's Symone.

"Want a gown?" I ask.

"No."

Sometimes Symone dresses up too. Other times she won't. Her show is finished and she says she's hungry. But after we eat, she will put on a gown, she says. So we make tuna sandwiches that I cut into little slices. Mother calls them finger sandwiches. Sometimes she makes them for her friends. Symone gets a bottle of iced tea and two china teacups with purple flowers on the inside. She sits them on a tray and carries everything into the living room.

"You be the slave," I tell her.

"No! *You* be the slave."

"I have on a gown." I lift my left foot. "And special shoes." I turn in circles so my gown floats. "And I'm the queen. A queen can't be a slave."

Symone walks over to me slow and sits the tray on a stool next to the couch. I ask her to wait while I go to my room and pick out a crown to match my dress. When I'm back, she hands me a saucer with a finger sandwich on it.

"I think I need something sweet, if you don't mind."

She knows where everything in our house is. She comes back with *arroz con dulce*, rice pudding with coconut milk, cinnamon, and raisins. Symone's mother made it. It's my favorite dessert. "Thank you. I will take my tea now."

I like being a queen because people have to do what you say. "Fill it to the top, please, and don't spill, not one drop."

She carries the tea over to me very carefully. She smiles and bows real low, the way I like. "Your Majesty, if it pleases the queen, may I put a drop of vanilla in your tea? It will make it tasty sweet."

"Indeed . . . please."

Symone reaches for the glass she brought back from the kitchen. She splashes a drop of vanilla into my cup.

"Hmmm, I smell it already." I set the cup on the tray and take a baby bite of my sandwich. "Queens have the best manners," I tell her. When Symone tries to sit down, I stop her. "Slaves can't sit. They can only stand."

She doesn't like that, but she stands while I eat.

I take my cup and blow. And sip. And spit tea on mother's dress and sofa. "It tastes like, like . . ."

"No better for you." Symone picks up a sandwich and bites into it. "I poured vinegar in your cup." Her mouth is open while she talks and eats. "You're a mean queen. And you know what happens to mean queens?"

I think about the queens my father told me about. How some ended up with no heads, poisoned, or locked in towers for all eternity.

"It's just pretend," I say.

The downstairs door to our building opens and closes. It's Mother, I bet, coming back from the store. Symone picks up her cup and sips. "I want to be queen." Her baby finger sticks out. "And *I* need a crown, a big one."

Nobody can wear my crowns except me. But Symone says if I don't let her wear one, she will tell Mother how I tried to make her into a slave. I am wondering why she is being like this. But then I remember what Mother said once: "If you spend too much time with friends, you may not be friends for very long." Symone has stayed too long at our house. That's why she's being rude.

Mother walks into the room and says hello. She asks if we are having a good time. Symone looks at me and smiles, then sticks out her hand. I reach for my crown right when Symone tells Mother that she would like to speak with her in private for a moment.

"Here," I say, throwing the crown at her, hoping she will keep quiet about me asking her to be my slave.

CHAPTER 9

SYMONE TALKS TOO MUCH. At first she told her mother what happened at my place. Her mother called my parents. Mother and Father didn't like what I did. They took away my crowns—for a month! They didn't let me have my books, or allow Father to read me any stories about queens. And when my brother's package came, they held on to it, even though they didn't know what was inside. "It has something to do with queens, crowns, and candy," Mother said. "Like always."

Father is usually on my side. Not this time. He said he was ashamed of me. "Symone is your friend. Not your flunky."

Symone is messing things up at school for me, too. She makes up stories about me. "She tried to make me a slave," she tells everyone. "She wanted me to bark like a dog and eat cake off the floor."

Why is she making things up about me? I ask her. She stands right there with everyone listening and says it is all true.

We are best friends. Best friends are nice to each other. I don't understand why she's not being nice to me. I said I was sorry. I told her she could come over my house and play dress up. She said she was never speaking to me again.

"A slave is not the worst thing you can be," I tell her.

She almost socks me for that. "Then what is the worst thing you can be?"

"Stupid. The worst thing you can be is stupid. My dad even says so."

She is thinking about what I said. I can tell.

I'm thinking about her, wondering why she's being like this. If she asked me to be her slave, I wouldn't do it. But I wouldn't be mad at her for asking.

Symone walks away from me, even though the other kids say she should punch me for what I did to her. I follow her. "Don't be . . ."

She waits until we're by the fence and nobody else is around. "You are stupid for thinking that you are better than everyone else."

"I don't think that I'm better than you."

"Then why did you try to make me be your slave?"

It was pretend. That's what I want to say. But she doesn't give me a chance to say it.

"You get the best dresses. You only want to play at your house. You get higher grades. You don't walk to school and . . ."

I'm trying to talk. She won't let me.

"AND I AM NOT YOUR SLAVE!"

"Okay!"

"Okay!"

"So we are friends again?" I ask, because if Symone is not my friend, it will make me sad because she is my only best friend, ever.

"Yeah, we are friends again."

I hug her. She squeezes me back. "I got gum," I say, pulling out a pack and handing it to her.

"This is my favorite kind," she says, taking as many as she wants.

CHAPTER 10

SHOW-AND-TELL is mostly for little kids. But Mrs. McBride makes us do it anyhow. I brought in my favorite crown. She wouldn't let me talk about it, though. She said it was the fourth time in a row that I had brought the same crown in. That's not so. I brought in three different crowns before: a clear plastic one that my aunt sent me from New Mexico, a golden one with purple and green stones from New Orleans, and a blue one with gray tips from Philadelphia.

"A crown is a crown is a crown," Mrs. McBride says. Then she tells me to go back to my seat. "You must have something else to show besides crowns."

I stare at my feet.

She walks over to me and bends down. "Don't you play with dolls? Don't you have games?" She looks like she feels sorry for me!

I shake my head no. The other kids laugh.

"Don't you have a favorite book?"

Before I can answer, Leroy's hand goes up.

"Yes, Leroy?"

Since Leroy came to our school three months ago, he is Mrs. McBride's new pet. She walks over to him and squeezes his cheeks.

"I have something to show," he says.

"Good. Take your place at the front of the class."

Leroy has a blue plastic bag in his hands. It's so heavy he carries it by the top and bottom. When he walks by, kids hold their noses and say he needs a bath.

Mrs. McBride's mouth gets so big you could stick a whole sandwich in it. "Quiet!"

Leroy smiles, like he can't hear those kids at all. He sits the bag on the desk and opens it.

"Ooh," we all say, standing up.

Sharon walks up to the front of the class without even asking permission. "Can I touch it?"

Mrs. McBride makes her sit back down. "Leroy, where did you get this?"

He tells her a big fat fib. "From Africa. My father . . ."

Mrs. McBride walks to the front of the class. She picks up the elephant tusk and sets it back down. Then she looks inside a small brown bag and holds it up to Leroy. She looks at him. Her mouth opens and closes three times in a row. "I will ask you again. Where did you get these?"

We are not supposed to leave our seats without permission. But when the gold coins fall out of the bag and roll across the floor, we chase after them. I pick up two coins. They are heavy, golden yellow. I stick one in my mouth and bite down on it like they do on television. It isn't filled with chocolate. It's hard and tastes like rust. It's real gold.

Mrs. McBride asks Leroy again where he got those things. He only makes it worse for himself, because she knows, just like I do, that he isn't a prince. That he's never been to Senegal. And that the gold coins and baby elephant tusk that he says was his great-great-grandfather's is no such thing. But he is standing there anyhow, telling her fib after fib. And right away she looks at me and says I have filled his head with foolishness. "So now we have a prince and a queen—all in one room. Oh, help me." She shakes her head and covers her face with her hands. Then she reaches for Leroy's chin. She stares into his eyes and says for him to tell her the truth. Only, before he can answer, she picks up something else from the desk. A small bottle filled with pink stuff.

Leroy reaches for it. "It's sand, from Cameroon. That's in Africa too." He picks up another bottle. It is filled with black grains. He says that's sand too. He takes off the top and puts the little bottle up to his ear. "You can hear the ocean if you listen hard."

That's it. Mrs. McBride slams her hand down on the desk. "No more fibs, Leroy." She looks at me like I'm the one telling tales. "No more stories about queens and kings. I mean princes." She marches over to me and snatches the coins from my fingers. Then she asks Leroy again to tell the truth or go to the principal's office.

"In Africa . . ."

She doesn't want to hear any more, I guess. She throws the sand bottles into the bag, not even putting the top back on. She takes Leroy by the arm and pulls him over to the door. "You come along too, Your Royal Highness," she says, looking back at me. Mrs. McBride says she is sure I had something to do with all this. "Probably put him up to it." She waits for me to come over to her. Her hands are on her hips and her lips are twisted. "Young lady, I want this foolishness to stop." She takes me to the principal's office right along with Leroy.

I try to tell her that I don't believe Leroy either. But when I go to speak, she puts her finger up to her lips. That means for me to keep quiet. I talk anyhow. Low, so she doesn't hear. But Leroy does. "Leroy Wright," I say, "I don't like you, not one little bit."

CHAPTER 11

I LIKE GOING to the principal's office. I like sitting in the big, soft, brown chairs and listening to the copy machine run and the phones ring. But mostly I like going because I get to see my name up on the wall. It's on beige poster board, right along with all the other students who never miss school and get good grades. My name is always first, though, because I get the most A's and I am the only student in school who has never ever missed a day of school in the two years I've been here.

"One, three, seven . . ."

Leroy stares up at the wall right along with me. "What are you counting?"

"Eight, nine." My finger follows all the gold and silver stars lined up beside my name. "I'm counting my stars. I have the most, more than anyone else in the whole school."

Leroy starts counting too. "Jeff's got the same amount as you."

I push his hand down. "That's because you don't know how to count." I count Jeff's stars. "Eight. Nine." I sit down with my arms crossed and my lips tight. My feet tap the floor as hard and fast as sticks hitting a drum.

The secretary with the blue hair stands up with her finger waving side to side. "Cut that out, young lady!"

I whisper, "Jeff's got green stars. Green ones don't count."

Leroy is playing with a pencil he found on the floor, rolling it across his forehead. He says green must count because it's on the wall, and if it didn't count it wouldn't be up there. I ask the secretary what the green stars mean. She says for me and Leroy to stop worrying about stars and be quiet. She's mad, I guess, because she was on the phone talking when I asked the question. "Sorry."

Mrs. McBride comes out of the principal's office and goes back to class. Miss Sprits, the principal, walks over to us, smiling. She sticks her hand out, shaking mine first, then Leroy's. I curtsy. Leroy is a copycat. He bows. Miss Sprits says that she is glad to meet two young people with such good manners. "It's a joy to see."

I push Leroy out of the way when we walk behind her into her office. I've been here plenty of times, so I want to make sure I get the best seat. "Move, Leroy. Girls first."

It doesn't bother him. He walks in behind me and goes over to a table by the window. It has a giant puzzle on it. He sits on the floor, not the couch that's right behind the puzzle. I sit on a gray chair with gigantic pink and yellow dots on it.

Miss Sprits wears her locs in a long ponytail down to the middle of her back. When she passes, I reach out and touch them because they remind me of my mother's pretty hair.

"We can all sit over there if you like," the principal says, walking over to Leroy and sitting on the couch. "I like puzzles too." She picks up two pieces and hands one to him. "I think really smart people like to work puzzles."

I jump up from my chair. "I'm smart." I go over to the puzzle and pick up a handful of pieces. "I can finish puzzles faster than anybody."

Leroy is holding his puzzle piece up high. "How many pieces do you need to make a whole puzzle?"

"A lot," I say.

Miss Sprits butts in. "This puzzle has one thousand pieces. Some puzzles have lots of pieces, some have a few."

Leroy asks too many questions. "Do they make the whole picture first and then cut it into pieces?"

I push three pieces into the right spots. "That's a stupid question, Leroy." I stare at the piece in my hand. "Everybody knows you have to cut them up first."

The principal leans over his shoulder. "There is no such thing as a stupid question." She pinches his cheek. "The more questions a student asks, the better I like it." She watches Leroy press a flower into place with his thumb. She tells us how puzzles are made. She hands two more pieces to Leroy. "Queen," she says, reaching out to me, "let's see what you have."

She thinks I am intelligent and tells me so when I put another piece into place. She makes room for me on the couch and talks to Leroy again. "You're very bright as well, so I know it's not possible that you stole anything."

Leroy keeps putting pieces into the puzzle. He repeats what he told everyone in class. He *is* really from Africa, and the sand and money are really his. Miss Sprits looks at me and asks why I'm in her office.

Leroy answers. "Mrs. McBride doesn't like her."

Miss Sprits coughs.

Leroy sits up straight. "She likes me, though. Every day she calls on me in class. Every day she says, 'Leroy, will you help me erase the blackboard? Will you collect the books and hand out paper?'"

Mrs. McBride does no such thing. The principal doesn't believe him either, I bet, because she interrupts him by getting up and going over to the phone on her desk. She is calling his mother. "It's not that I don't believe you, Leroy. It's just that I have to double-check these kinds of things."

Leroy is sitting on the floor working the puzzle, not even caring that he is smelling up her office. Not even caring that he got me into trouble for no real reason.

"Yes," I hear the principal say. "Well, he does say that they are his. Only . . ."

She isn't on the phone long. She comes back over to us, smiling. "Well, Mr. Wright, I believe these belong to you." She sets the bag of coins, sand, and the elephant tusk on the table next to Leroy. She says his mother must really love him to trust him with such wonderful treasures. She pats Leroy's cheek like he is the best little boy in the world. "One day you will have to come visit me again and tell me all about Africa."

Leroy's still on the floor, not even looking up at Miss Sprits. "You may keep them," he says, picking up another puzzle piece. "I have plenty."

CHAPTER 12

"I DON'T WANT TO GO, but they are making me." Symone is crying. I am crying. Her mother and my mother are crying. We are all at my house, hugging and crying together.

Her *abuela*, grandmother, is sick—old and sick and living by herself in Puerto Rico. Last week she slipped in the bathtub and hurt her hip. Now Symone and her mom have to go and take care of her. They will leave tomorrow and come back in three months. Symone will go to school there.

"You already know how to talk like they do."

"*Sí,*" she says. "I have been speaking Spanish since I was, um, *pequeña.*"

"What?" I ask.

"Since I was little."

Mother and Mrs. Santiago drink coffee and talk. Symone could stay at our house, that's what Mother keeps telling her. But Symone's mom says no. They may be gone longer than she thinks. "Three months could turn into ten months if her hip doesn't heal properly."

"I'm going to miss my favorite TV shows," Symone says, sitting on my bed and aiming the clicker at the set. "And my favorite bubble gum." She blows a big, purple bubble. I smash it and we both pick gum off her nose.

After lunch, I sit next to her, holding out my hands and asking her to guess what is in each one. She taps my right hand. I open it.

"You're giving those to me? Your favorite crown earrings?"

They are not my *favorite* earrings. They look like them, though. Only, sometimes the crown falls off the left one, and you can lose it if you aren't careful. "I'm giving them to you so you don't forget about me."

She touches my other hand. When it opens, I show her a small book of stamps and a pack of crown stickers. "So you will write to me."

Symone squeezes me with hugs. I squeeze back. She leaves the room and comes back with a gift wrapped in burgundy tissue paper and white ribbon. I open it slowly. It's a photo album, a little one, with pictures of her, me, and our moms.

"Don't forget me," she says, covering her face.

"I won't have any friends after you go."

Symone digs in her back pocket and pulls out a piece of paper. "Here. I almost forgot."

Dear Queen,
When I am gone, be nice. Don't ask people to be your slave. Don't talk about your shoes and crowns all the time. Don't know everything in class or get mad so much.
And don't forget about me.
Symone, your best friend ever!!!

I take the letter and put it in my box of special things. "I won't forget."

Mother calls us in for cake and ice cream. While she is setting the table, Symone and I go to the balcony and people-watch. I wave to people I know, and she and I laugh at a man standing on a box playing a violin with a green parrot sitting on his shoulder.

"Ooh," Symone says, "that girl is taking some of his money."

She's right. A girl with pink hair takes dollar bills from the violin case on the ground and runs up the street. The man keeps playing, but the bird's screaming, "Crook! Thief! Cops! Crook! Thief! Cops!"

The bird makes us laugh.

Mother calls us into the kitchen to eat.

"Crook," I say.

"Thief!" Symone yells.

"Cops," we say, holding hands and skipping into the kitchen for treats.

CHAPTER 13

EVERYBODY LIKES LEROY NOW. He still smells the same. Still has holes in his pants and run-over shoes, but for three whole weeks everyone has wanted to be his friend. They listen to his stories about picking yams in Senegal and selling peanuts on the streets there. They ask him to teach them how to speak French; so does Mrs. McBride!

The kids take up for him, too. If I walk over to him, James will ask me what I want. Then he pushes me or yells for me to "Leave Leroy alone and stop being so mean to everybody!"

At lunchtime the other day I read a letter from my brother Joshua. He said maybe I should try and make a new friend now that Symone is gone. So that's what I'm trying to do. After lunch I go over to some girls jumping rope. I ask if I can turn. One girl, Rachel, makes a face. "No. Go away." I get angry and tell her I don't want to play with them anyhow. "Besides, that's not a real rope," I say, biting on a purple candy-crown necklace Father bought me. "It's just a clothesline you found in the trash somewhere."

They chase me with that rope. Mrs. McBride said I was getting what I deserved for that big mouth of mine. But she lets me stand beside her anyhow, and she tells the girls to leave me alone. For five whole days afterward, I stand by her and eat my lunch and then watch the others run around having fun.

I want friends. I want kids to like me. It's just, well, they are jealous of me. They know I know more than they do, and they don't like that. They know I have the prettiest shoes and the nicest earrings, and that's why they pick on me. Only, having the best stuff and knowing the biggest words isn't all that much fun if you don't get to tell anybody about them.

On the way home from school the other day, I stopped Leroy and told him he'd better be my friend or else. He laughed. I told Mother what I did. She laughed too. She said that you cannot make people be friends with you. I guess she's right. So I will stop trying to make people like me. This morning I came up with a better idea. I will follow Leroy home and find out the truth about him. Then I will tell everybody what I know. When they see that he's a fake, they will stop liking him and like me.

I like to spy on people. To catch them doing what they shouldn't. Today I'm following Leroy home. He's on that bike, singing, clapping his hands, and waving to strangers—riding as slow as a turtle. Not even paying attention to me. So I walk way behind him, tying my shoestring every time he does something ridiculous like stop to put rocks in his pockets.

I am following Leroy because I don't know exactly which apartment he lives in, even though he lives in the projects across the street from me. It takes him forever to get home. But he still doesn't know I'm behind him until he's off his bike and walking inside building number three. I don't move when the door closes behind him. I wait. Then open it quietly. I tiptoe up the stairs behind him, like a thief trying not to get caught. He stops in the stairwell leading to the third floor. That's when I holler for him to wait up. He wants to know why I'm here. And he doesn't ask it very nicely.

I open my backpack and spread clean papers on the top step. Then I sit down. "I want to meet your mother." I puff out my new skirt and stare at the sneakers I got from my brother Marcus yesterday.

For twenty minutes Leroy just sits next to me, not talking. That's okay, I tell him, because Mother's not home and I can stay here all night— which is not true at all.

When Leroy is tired of waiting, he walks over to apartment 310, using his key to get inside. He makes me stand in the hallway forever. Finally the door opens and closes quickly five times in a row.

Then a woman pushes it open wide. She is wearing a long red gown with gold threads running through it, and her hair is wrapped tight with orange cloth as tall as the pot Mother cooks Christmas collard greens in.

"You Leroy's mother?"

"I am," she says, looking down at me like she is somebody important and I'm not.

I stare at her fingers. She is wearing six rings. One has an emerald—my mother's birthstone. I look down at her feet. She has on fuzzy slippers.

"You ever live in Africa? Owned a palace?"

She isn't very nice. "That ain't your . . . well, if Leroy says I did, I did." She clears her throat. "I mean, yes. We have been to many places."

I ask her about the elephant tusk and the gold coins. "How'd you get them? Did somebody steal them for you?"

She looks like she wants to slap me. "Leroy told you, didn't he?" Before I can answer, the door is closing. "So why are you asking me what you already know?"

Just like that the door flies open again, and Leroy's mother is smiling this time. Her lips move, but no words come out at first, like maybe she is talking to herself, or practicing what she wants to say. She bends down to my size, holding my hands in hers. "*Mes excuses, ma petite.* It's been so long since I've been back home, I've forgotten my manners. You agree?" She stares at Leroy. He shakes his head up and down. Her hand pats me on the head.

"Does Leroy have a brother named Chop?" I bend down, trying to look inside their apartment. "Is he in there? Tell him to come out."

Leroy's mom taps her foot and counts to ten. She says she must go, before her food burns. Without even saying good-bye, she slams the door shut.

I walk to the stairwell, thinking about her gown and rings. About how tall she is and how her hands and body move like there is soft, sweet music playing deep inside her.

I pick restaurant flyers off the floor and stuff them in the trash. Maybe, I think, things can happen, and a queen could lose her castle and have to live in a place with trash on the floor.

I look both ways before I cross the street. I feel

bad, though. I wanted people to not like Leroy, to see that he was fibbing about everything. Only, now I'm not so sure. Maybe he is a prince, even if he smells like pee.

When I get home, Mother asks where I've been. I pretend that I am telling the truth. "Visiting Mrs. Jefferson downstairs."

She tells me to wash for dinner. I skip all the way to the bathroom. But right before I step on my fluffy purple rug, I remember the bunny rabbits. "Her fuzzy slippers had purple rabbits on them," I say, thinking about Leroy's mom. "A real queen would never wear those."

Mother asks why I am so happy when I skip back into the living room. I can't tell her. She wouldn't think it was very nice.

CHAPTER 14

A FAKE QUEEN, that's what Leroy's mother is. I don't tell him what I know. I keep it to myself, and a few days later I follow him home again. This time he rides his bike to the store and comes out with blue grocery bags. The bags hang from his handlebars, so he stops and rests a lot. When he gets inside, he doesn't go to his apartment. He knocks on another door and a man answers. "Here, Cornelius. I brought everything you requested." He hands the man the bags.

"*Merci beaucoup, mon petit*. Thank you, my little one," the man says.

Leroy smiles. "*De rien.* You're welcome." He takes paper out of his back pocket and, reading from it, he says some more words in French, then puts it away. "I am doing good at learning to speak French, huh?" he says.

The man is tall and his voice is strong and deep. "*Très bien.* Excellent. You're a quick study and a good friend." Cornelius's voice goes low, but I hear him say my name, Queen, and the word "mean." Leroy thinks it's funny. They both laugh. The door opens wider and he goes inside. From where I'm standing I can see everything.

Why was Leroy talking to a stranger about me? How did this man know that people called me mean? And why is he teaching Leroy French, when Leroy tells everyone he spoke French way back home?

Mother says if I want the answers to questions, all I have to do is ask. So I bang on the man's door. I don't care if he doesn't like it. I don't care if Leroy gets angry, either. They have no right to talk about me behind my back.

The door opens. "Scat!"

I jump back.

The man talks funny, like he's from another country. "Didn'tie tell ya—scat? Me don't be liking company."

He slams the door, and it feels like the whole building shakes. I knock again, calling Leroy's name. This time Leroy comes to the door, just standing there with his lips pocked out at me. I'm glad, because now I get to see inside Cornelius's place. It's a sight.

"Leroy."

He shuts the door behind him. "Shhhh."

I go to knock one more time. Leroy stops me. He tells me not to go ruining things for him. I let him know that it's rude, slamming doors in people's faces. Even grown-ups don't have a right to do that. And queens especially don't like doors slammed. Leroy tells me again not to mess things up for him. So I don't knock. I take off my backpack and drop it on the floor. I sit on it and ask him about that man and his messy house.

"It's funky." I lick my lips. "From all those cats."

Leroy doesn't pay me any mind.

"How many cats does he have?"

He sits down on the floor. "I don't know. Ten, maybe."

He wasn't fibbing this time. I saw cats on the couch, a calico cat in the windowsill sleeping, and more cats lying on the rug, sitting on the TV, sleeping on the floor, and rubbing against the door. "I like cats. Mother won't let me have any, though."

"He doesn't go looking for 'em. They just show up, like magic." Leroy walks over to the door and puts his ear to it. "You ruin everything."

"What did I do?"

He gets closer to me. I don't like that. He smells. Like, like cats! Like a million cats that never get washed. "You smell like them," I say, staring at the door. I fan my nose and let out a sneeze the size of Mrs. McBride's U.S. wall map. *"Aaa choo!"*

"Bless you."

"Aaaa, choo!"

"Bless you twice."

"Aaaa, choo!"

"Bless you once. Bless you twice. Next time I won't be so nice," Leroy says, plucking my nose like kids do in school when they get tired of blessing you.

I am glad, kinda, to know that Leroy doesn't smell because he never washes. But who would want to be in a house with so many cats?

I let Leroy know that I am not leaving until he tells me who the man is and how come he is teaching him French. Leroy starts making things up, I think, because it doesn't make sense. He says Cornelius is famous. That he has been around the world and speaks four languages. I want to sock Leroy for not telling the truth. I mean, anyone can see that the man is poor. I saw his place. Cans of cat food everywhere. Newspapers piled up like shirts that need ironing. A silver Christmas tree leaning against a wall. And lots and lots of boxes— shoe boxes, jewelry boxes, computer boxes, litter boxes.

"How'd you see all that through a little crack in the door?" Leroy asks.

I tell him that I'm good at puzzle books where you find what doesn't belong, so it's easy for me to see when things don't look right. I put my backpack on, reach in my pocket, and put on my double crown pinky ring. I point to my head. "I think he's missing something up here."

Leroy tells me to get.

"Bet he stole all those cats."

He lets me know not to ever come here again. "You always cause trouble. That's why Cornelius didn't open the door."

"Cornelius is a stupid name."

"He could tell . . ." Leroy starts shoving me. "He could tell that you were all slimy and stinky inside." He pokes me. I poke him back. He shoves me, so I do the same. "Get out!" he shouts. "You mess up everything!"

I look down the stairs. The light is out. The hallway is as dark as nighttime. "Leroy."

He turns his back to me.

I swallow. *A queen is never afraid*, I hear Father say. *She is brave and strong and true.*

I straighten myself up, fix my invisible crown, and walk down the steps, telling myself what a wonderful, smart, pretty girl I am.

CHAPTER 15

THE NEXT DAY when I see Leroy at school, he is sitting on the ground reading a book. I am nicer to him this time. "What ya reading?"

He turns around. "Nothing."

I never sit on the ground, so I take out a piece of notebook paper and sit on it. "*The Book of Big Things*," I say, reading the title. "That sounds like a baby book."

Leroy gets up and moves.

I follow him. He tells me to go away. I stop. He walks over to some boys, and the next thing I know they are chasing each other. Running and bumping into everybody. I watch. All during lunch period nobody else even talks to me. When we line up to go to class, Leroy jumps in front of me. "I'm sorry," I whisper.

His hair is tight brown balls that never get combed. But his smile gets big when he tells me, "That's all right. You can't help it if you were born mean." He turns back around and we all walk inside behind Mrs. McBride.

I keep touching Leroy's shoulder, trying to let him know I wasn't born mean. That I'm not mean at all. He ignores me. When we get inside, I pass him a note.

"I'll take that." Mrs. McBride reads my note and frowns. "You think mighty much of yourself, now don't you, young lady?"

I keep hoping she won't read the note out loud. She doesn't. She folds it up and asks us to take out our reading books. Feet move and papers crumble. Hands go up. I wave mine too. Only, Mrs. McBride never calls on me. "I know all the answers," I say under my breath.

"So?" a girl sitting next to me says. "Nobody cares what you know."

When school is out, I go up to Mrs. McBride and ask for my note. She takes it out of her drawer and says for me not to pass notes in class. "Queen," she says, sitting on the edge of her desk, "you are a smart girl—"

I don't let her finish. "I know."

Mrs. McBride's face gets red. "But sometimes . . ."

"I'm smarter than everyone here, and you never call on me." I fold the note and stick it in my pocket. "It hurts my feelings."

She covers her face with her hands and rubs her poppy eyes. "A queen should be humble. You know what the word 'humble' means?"

I tell her that I read on a seventh-grade level so of course I know what the word means.

"Oh," she says. "I should have known."

"Will you call on me tomorrow? Just once?"

She gets up and walks the aisles, picking trash off the floor, opening desks and stuffing papers inside. "Maybe. Maybe I will call on you," she says, stopping to rub her temples.

I know that means no. Only, I don't let on what I'm thinking. I reach into my pocket and pull out my gold crown key chain. "A queen's subjects don't always like her," I say, repeating what I heard on TV once.

Mrs. McBride doesn't like that. She folds her arms so tight they look stuck. "I am not your subject." She points to the empty chairs. "These kids are not your subjects either." She puts her hands on my shoulders. "And as long as you think they are your subjects—people to boss around and scorn—they will never be your friends."

My bottom lip starts shaking and my nose won't stop dripping. Maybe that's why Mrs. McBride makes a deal with me. She says that she and I will start all over again, like it was the first day of class. As if she never set eyes on me before. "Now, what is your name?" she asks, smiling.

"Queen Rosseau," I say, and before I can catch myself, I say something to ruin everything and make her not like me all over again. "And you may bow to me if you like."

Mrs. McBride has a lot of red faces: light red when she laughs, red like raspberry tea when she cries, and red like cherries when she is extra mad. She is cherry red, so I don't wait for her to tell me to leave. I walk out the classroom door. I might have stayed sad all the way home, only right after I shut the door, I see Leroy. He is waiting for me, he says. Right then, I know that Mrs. McBride doesn't know what she's talking about. I do have friends: one, anyhow.

CHAPTER 16

LEROY MAKES ME PROMISE to keep my big mouth shut. I promise. For the next seven blocks, it's just him talking, telling me all about Cornelius Junction the Fourth. I want to tell him to stop making up stories. But the more he talks, the more I think maybe, just maybe, Leroy Wright is telling the truth, for once.

Leroy isn't riding his bike today. His mother made him leave it home. "I went to the store for

Cornelius the other day, and there were some puppies all by themselves. I stayed with them until
their mother came. It was dark when I got home.
My mother didn't like that.

"Cornelius used to be in plays on Broadway,"
Leroy says, forgetting about the puppies. He stops
walking and asks if I know that's a place in New
York City where people act onstage. Of course I
know. I know everything. Leroy won't shut up. He
says that Cornelius has all kinds of accents. Some
days he sounds like a cowboy. Other times he
sounds like those people from Africa. "The gold is
his."

Fake, I say in my head.

"He's got sand from Africa, seashells from
Greece, and a little bitty Eiffel Tower from France."

You can get that junk anywhere, I tell myself.
But I never say anything to Leroy, because I don't
want him to not be my friend again.

Leroy is talking and talking. Saying Cornelius
used to live in San Francisco, New Mexico,
London, Singapore, Beijing, and Mississippi too.

Pretty pictures of some of those places pop into
my head, and I wonder if I will get to travel the

world like that someday. "If he's such a big deal, how did he end up here, living in the projects?"

We are walking up the street. Talking too long at lights and missing them. Leroy whispers, like maybe Cornelius will hear. "One day, all of a sudden, he was too scared to act in front of people. Then he got afraid to leave his porch, and too frightened to leave his house." Leroy knows a lot about Cornelius, like how he had to move into Leroy's building a few years ago when all his money ran out.

I feel sorry for Cornelius. He is tall like my father and has big arm muscles. But inside he must be as scared as a cat being chased by a pit bull, that's what I figure, anyhow.

Leroy reaches for my hand when we cross the street. "Oh, he's all right now. Thanks to me," he says, rubbing his head. "I go to the store for him. Buy whatever's on the list that he gives me." He looks both ways, making sure the cars are stopped before we step into the street. "Anyhow, I've been telling Cornelius about you."

I stand still. "Me?"

He pulls me by my arm. "I tell him that you're

always talking about being a queen. That you wear crowns and act stuck-up and—"

"I'm not stuck-up."

He keeps talking. "Cornelius says that a queen doesn't have to live in a real castle."

I stop walking.

"That you only gotta believe in your head that you're a queen." He looks at me. "He says it doesn't matter what anybody else thinks. It only matters what you think of yourself."

I pretend he's saying that in front of Mrs. McBride. "Told ya I was a queen," I say to Leroy. But inside I'm really saying it to her.

He smacks his chest. "I'm a prince."

"No you're not! And you've never been to Africa, either!"

"Cornelius—"

"Cornelius isn't anybody but a scaredy-cat, too afraid to step outside his own front door."

Leroy's eyes look at me like he's never seen me before. "People say bad things about Cornelius, but when my mom and I run out of food, he knows. Grocery bags appear outside our door."

I try to say I'm sorry. He won't let me.

"It's not cheap food. It's good stuff, steaks and chops, hamburger meat piled up to the ceiling. All the stuff we like."

"Leroy."

He is walking away from me. Turning around quick, he says, "I did live in Africa!"

"But—"

"And I've seen the ocean with the pink sand, touched the Pyramids with my hand, and swam in the Zambezi River in my drawers." Leroy walks in circles. "My mother, my mother is a queen. A real one. A nice one, not like you." He tells me her name, and says his dad really did put them on a ship to save their lives.

He walks over to me and pushes me hard. "And Cornelius, he is nicer than you any day," he says, crossing the street and leaving me behind.

CHAPTER 17

WHEN FATHER AND I WALK out the door, we see Leroy riding his bike down the hill. He waves at Father, puts his arms high in the air, and rolls down the hill yelling at the top of his lungs.

Father shuts the car door behind me. "Let's invite him to dinner tonight."

I tell him that Leroy won't come. But when we get to school, Father goes over to him. He shakes Leroy's hand and tells him his bike needs a little fixing up. "Rust isn't permanent, you know. That pedal, that seat." He shakes the bike like he wants something to fall off. "Well, you don't have much of a seat. But I could pick a new one up someplace. Put it on." He squeezes the tires. "The rust can be sanded off, and a new coat of paint put on."

Every word out of Father's mouth makes Leroy's smile bigger. "What're y'all cooking?"

"Don't know. You'll just have to take your chances."

Leroy and my father shake hands again. "Okay," Leroy says, ignoring me and riding away.

"He doesn't like me," I mumble.

"A queen . . ."

"I'm not a queen. My name is Queen but I'm not a real queen. Everyone says so." I try not to cry. And I don't tell him about what happened last week with Leroy, or Mrs. McBride and me. For sure I don't tell him what Symone wrote to me in her last letter, saying that she will be gone longer than she thought, and that she found a new best friend, Abrigaila, so I couldn't be her best friend anymore.

Father whispers. "You are a queen. My queen. Beautiful. Smart. Wonderful." He makes me look him in the eyes. "Queens can make the world better. They can make people feel all warm and safe inside." He kisses my nose. "They don't have to hurt people with words or make them feel unimportant."

I put my backpack over one shoulder and kiss him good-bye. I want to be nice to people. I want them to like me, only it always goes wrong. The words come out as hard and crooked as Melnick Washmiller's front tooth. But right after my father drives off, I make up my mind. From now on I'm going to be nice to people.

CHAPTER 18

"IN AFRICA, WE EAT with our toes some-times."

I know that isn't true. But I don't say anything when Leroy tells us that.

"And we, we . . ." Leroy is trying to think up more fibs. My parents don't even try to make him stop. They keep asking questions and laughing at everything he says. I am trying to be nice, so I don't talk all that much. But if I were going to talk, I would say, "Leroy! Shut up. Stop fibbing. Go home and take a bath."

My mother made baked chicken and rice. She waited until Leroy came and then she made biscuits. She asked if he wanted to help. She made me go into the dining room and set the table. She asked him about school and his mother. She got him to put hot water in the Jell-O and let him pour it in the molds. I folded the napkins and put the plates on the table. She is being mean to me, and I don't know why.

Mother pats his shoulder. "Leroy. You make me happy when you eat my food."

Leroy stuffs more food in his mouth. "Mmm," he says. "Your food makes my mouth dance."

"Don't forget. I will pack a bag for your mother and you to eat later on."

"Can I get four slices of cake to take home with me?"

Mother and Father laugh. I don't. He's being rude, wanting all of our food for himself. Only, I don't say anything. I'm being nice, smiling even when I don't want to.

"Ready?" Father asks him.

Leroy jumps up and wipes his fingers on his shirt. "My bike's out front."

Father takes his plate to the sink. He puts on his overalls, gets his toolbox, then he and Leroy go outside. They don't come back for hours. By then, Mother and I have the table cleared and the dishes washed. I am doing my homework. Leroy comes up to say good night to Mother. But he doesn't say one word to me. All the time he's there, he doesn't even say my name. Mother and Father let him get away with it too. When I ask them about it later, they say they hadn't noticed.

For the next ten days Leroy has dinner with us. He eats all the good stuff and takes home all the leftovers. He and Father paint the bike. They put on a new red seat. Replace the tires. Screw on a loud, silver horn and change the pedals. They do everything together, and they do it without me.

So I read. And I get madder and madder at Leroy. He laughs louder when he is with my parents. His fibs are bigger. And he always finds a way to get extra hugs and kisses from my mom.

The whole time he's at our place, he hardly talks to me. He just says, "Pass the potatoes, please," or "Queen, can you move your foot so I can get by?"

Every day I say to myself, *Kick him. Hit him with something hard.* But I don't. I do something kind instead. I bring him napkins without anyone asking me. I refill his glass with ice and run down the stairs to open the door when he rings the bell right after school. I even tried out my niceness on the kids at school. "Thank you, Queen," Markeeta said after I picked her monster-head pencil up off the floor today. Mrs. McBride was so proud of me that she gave me a hug and let me answer a question before I even raised my hand.

I was even nicer at lunch. I made sure Mrs. McBride saw me, because sometimes she will give kids treats for behaving well. "Here." I broke my cheese sandwich in half and put part of it on Bobbie's lunch box.

He picked it up and sat it on the table. "I hate cheese."

Being nice is hard work. But I kept at it. "I have chocolate milk. Want a sip?"

"No."

Mrs. McBride was smiling at me, so I kept

offering him other things. "Do you want my carrots?"

"No."

"How about raisins?"

"Naw."

"What about my apple?"

"Nope."

Mrs. McBride went over to talk to a teacher.

"Take something," I said, pulling his fingers over to my food.

Bobbie is a crybaby. He screamed like I was breaking his arm. "Stop hurting my arm!"

Mrs. McBride didn't hear, because everyone in the lunchroom talks so loud. I told Bobbie if he ate some of my food, and told Mrs. McBride how good I was at sharing, I would give him a dollar. Leroy heard me say that. And like it was his business, he told me that you cannot buy friendship. Naturally, Mrs. McBride had just come back, and she heard him. She waved her finger at me. "Queen, Leroy is telling you right. Friends aren't toys that you can buy."

Mrs. McBride had a chocolate-chip cookie in her hand, the kind they sell at school only on

Tuesdays. She gave it to Leroy. After that, Leroy and Bobbie went out to play. By the time I got outside, everyone knew what I'd done. "Leroy Wright!" I screamed. "You have a big mouth!"

I tried to explain, but nobody listened. Nobody came over to play with me, either. At least Leroy should've come, for all the times he ate at my house for free. So I stayed by myself thinking—thinking a really long, long time. Till I came up with a great idea. I was going to stop being so nice! It doesn't work anyhow. Speaking to kids at school, picking up the pencils they drop, and sharing my lunch with them didn't get me one single new friend. And no matter how much I tried, Leroy still treated me like he didn't like me much. So I came up with a new plan. I will go to Cornelius's place tomorrow. I will knock until he answers. I will stay until he lets me in. And I will talk and talk and talk until he tells me the truth about Leroy Wright, who's never been to Africa, whose father is in no way a king, and whose mother is just a lady in two-dollar house slippers who doesn't know one single thing about being a queen.

CHAPTER 19

IT TAKES A COUPLE OF DAYS, but I finally get to go to Cornelius's place. I knock. He doesn't open the door. I kick it three times. He comes and tells me to go away, but the door is still shut. I remind him who I am. He doesn't care if I am the Queen of England. He says I'd better get away from his door before he calls the police. Two days later I come back. No answer.

I have a flashlight the next time I show up. I

knock on his door. He opens it. "What ya want, cowgirl?"

"Leroy says . . ."

"Leroy ain't your business."

"But . . ."

"Go away, little doggie."

I tell him I want to know if Leroy's ever been to Africa. He asks me if I've ever sat on a throne or lived in a castle.

"People say my house looks like a castle."

"Go away and stop pestering me."

"I'm just gonna come back."

"I'm just not gonna answer when you knock."

I go home and I don't come back for days.

Leroy practically lives at our house now. His bike is fixed, but every day he's at our place talking to Father. Naturally, it's suppertime when he comes by, so Mother has to invite him to stay. He is too big to sit in Mother's lap, but yesterday that's just what he did. Supper was over and I asked if Father could read a story. Sometimes when he reads to me I sit in his lap. That's what I did, right after I changed into my pur-ple silk pajamas and put on my crown-covered socks. Mother looked at Leroy, patted her thighs, and said she had room for him if he didn't mind being hugged and kissed. As big as he is, needing a bath and everything, Leroy jumped in her lap like he was a frog that had found the fattest lily pad in the kingdom.

I got so mad I couldn't listen to the story, or repeat my favorite parts right along with Father. So as soon as it ended, I went to bed. I didn't even let Father or Mother tuck me in. I was talking to myself, out loud, and I didn't want them to hear. "Leroy Wright, you won't think so mighty much of yourself after I tell people who you really are." I dreamed about Mrs. McBride standing him in front of the class, pinning a note to his chest: **Leroy Wright is a big, fat fake.**

Today, right after school, I'm back at Cornelius's place. I knock. I kick. I throw my heavy book bag up against his door. I yell and scream. Finally, after twenty minutes, the door opens just a little.

"Why, you spoiled little brat," he says, spit flying. "You have the manners of a pig."

CHAPTER 20

CORNELIUS CRACKS OPEN the door wider. I see more things this time. More cats. A couch shaped like a pair of big red lips, pictures of Cornelius that cover the entire living room wall. He's onstage, in different costumes. I have never, ever seen a person dressed in so many different outfits. I want to ask him about them, but he keeps talking.

"I be wanting to tell you a little somethin',

child," he says in a pretend accent. "You knock on me door again, and you be gettin' more trouble than you want."

He has on a hat. A tall, black, shiny hat that goes with a tuxedo, not the green plaid pants he's wearing. "Now, talk."

I tell him that Leroy is a fibber and I want to prove it.

His eyes roll. "Do Leroy be your business?"

I pretend that I have on my best, most beautiful, golden yellow crown. I stand straight and speak clearly. "People shouldn't lie."

"Cowboys and girls," he says, spinning his arm in the air like he's gonna rope something, "saddle up! It's rodeo time."

I stare at him, rocking back and forth like he's on a wooden horse. Cornelius is cuckoo, I think. So I take off. I'm almost down the first flight of steps when I hear him shout, "Who shot President Lincoln?"

I keep walking.

"Answer me, little queen."

I yell. "John Wilkes Booth. Everybody knows that."

"And where be Jamaica, child? In the U.S. or the Caribbean?"

"Easy, stupid questions," I say, walking backward up the steps. "The Caribbean."

He asks me something that stumps me. "Why the sand in some parts of Africa be pink, child? Huh? Huh? Huh?"

So there *is* pink sand in Africa. Leroy said it, Mother and Father too. Only, I didn't believe not one of them. And I didn't find out about it on the computer, so I thought they were just trying to make Leroy look smart.

"I think different, but I'm not out of my head." He acts weird, he says, to keep pests away. "So what makes sand pink?"

I don't have the answer. He stares at his watch. I stare inside his apartment, wondering. I can't answer, because I don't know. I tell him so. That's when he slams the door in my face.

CHAPTER 21

I TELL MOTHER I'M staying after school
to help Mrs. McBride wash the boards and clean
the erasers. She likes that. She says it's good that
I'm getting closer to my teacher. I am just telling
fibs. Every day now I go and visit with Cornelius.
I wait until Leroy is gone from his apartment. I
don't want him to know what I'm up to.

It's been two and a half weeks, and Cornelius
still won't let me inside.

"What you know new today?" he asks every time I come by.

"Nothing."

"Get out my face, then." *Slam* goes the door.

Then one day he says, "I don't be liking dumb people. You gonna talk with me, Cowgirl Jane, you best bring me something new every day." He throws a balled-up piece of paper at me. I open it. In words the size of ants, he's written down what he's learned all week. All the space on the front and back are filled up. There are two recipes and sixteen words I've never heard of. There's something about Russia, and a picture of an island, and the words "China has a Great Wall and I walked it barefooted when I was there." I can't read the rest of his writing. But I wonder: has he really been to China before? And what kind of wall did he walk on while he was there?

Before I leave, he tells me to come back with the names of five queens that ruled countries in Africa and three queens from England. I do it, but my father has to help me. "This doesn't seem like fifth-grade work to me," Father says.

The next day I knock on the door. "Cornelius, I

have the answers." He reads the paper I give him. He isn't talking today, just handing me a note filled with sand.

"A riddle?" I say, blowing away sand and reading.

Do this if you can
But don't use computer and forget
    about man
Use what the pillow lifts up, and the
    crown sits high upon
To answer this riddle you've set your
    sights on
They say that the Atlantic runs wide
    and deep
Past this country where yams grow
    under one's feet
It's a beautiful place where the car
    and the drum
Live side by side like your finger and
    your thumb
Stick your toes in the sand
Say hello to Maryland
Sip the coffee, cocoa too

Take a pineapple home with you
See Diana.
Like her hair?
Best not mention the word "zoo" if
    she is near.
Have you figured out this riddle?
Do you know the place, child?
Give me the answer, if you're able
'Cause it's the key to get inside*

I don't know what he's talking about. It's
gibberish. But long after I'm in bed I'm still trying
to figure it out. Even in my dreams, I am thinking.
I want to use the Internet, but the riddle says not
to. So I go to the encyclopedia, the dictionary, the
thesaurus, and the school library, too. Father asks
what I'm working on. I zip my lips. Every day after
school Mother looks over my shoulder. "What's
this? A special project?"

I don't say. I keep working to find the answer.

I am stumped for 24 days, 14 hours, and 56
minutes. When I do figure the riddle out, I run out
the house, across the street, and over to Cornelius's
place. "Here. I have the answer!"

"Well, well, well. You *are* as smart as you think you are."

I push his door open and go to step inside. He blocks me.

"You are invited in when I say you are invited in."

"But—"

"Good day, *ma petite*."

The door closes. I stand there with my answer in my hand. "But, but I got it right." I look at his riddle. The answer is the key to get inside. That's what it says.

The door stays shut anyhow.

CHAPTER 22

LEROY HANDS IT TO ME IN school—a printed invitation with my name engraved on top.

> *Queen Rosseau,*
> *You have found the key, so you are now cordially*
> *invited to visit with me.*
> *Cornelius Junction IV*

Leroy wants to know what the invitation says.

I don't tell. It's for my eyes only.

"I know you visit Cornelius," Leroy says, throwing stones in the air and catching 'em. "I'm not mad, though." He runs after James.

I wonder if Cornelius told on me, or if Leroy is spying on me the way I spied on him. I want to ask, but I don't. I open my invitation again and read it six times before I put it away.

I go to Cornelius's place right after school. I knock softly. He takes the chain off and opens the door wide enough for me to come inside. I'm scared. Mother says never go into a stranger's home. Only, Cornelius isn't a stranger now. He's my friend. My only one. So I go inside, stepping over cats and balls of gray fur. His place smells ten times worse than Leroy. I tell him so, too. But it's a nice place—like a museum or an antique shop.

First he asks me how I found the answer to his riddle. I take my time, explaining all the ways I went searching for it. "It was fun. Like a game."

He asks me how come I didn't quit. "It is a lot of work just to find the name of one African country," he says.

"You can't quit if you want to win. Anyhow, I

wanted to get into your house. So I couldn't give up."

He stares at me. "How many friends do you have, Queen?"

I move a pile of newspapers from a seat and sit down. "Plenty."

He laughs. "Mean queens can say and do as they like, but they can't make you be their friends."

Two brown cats with white paws jump into my lap. Three more rub my legs and walk over my feet like they are crossing the street. I am glad to be inside. Glad to get a really good look around. "Who cleans your place?" I lean back and stare at pictures of Cornelius with golden leaves around his head.

He walks over to me. "I clean my own place, and I've got extra soap for that mean mouth of yours." He pulls a bar of green soap from his pocket and hands it to me.

I shake my head no, and cover my lips with my fingers. "Sorry."

When Cornelius goes to the kitchen, I look around, stopping at a table full of statues and awards with his name on them. I check out the pictures on the walls. There are thirty-five of them—

all dusty—with the names of plays written under-neath. *The King and I. The Wiz. A Raisin in the Sun. Cats. Romeo and Juliet.*

His house smells different now, like chicken soup and raisin toast. I rub my belly and keep snooping. I never tell anyone anymore, but I want to be an actress when I grow up. It's the only way I can be all of the queens I like to read about. I told that to my brother Kingston once, and he said actresses don't make very much money. Father and Mother said the same thing, so I never mentioned it again. But that didn't change my mind. I still like it when everyone around me is looking at me and thinking I'm special.

Just when I go to investigate other things, I hear Cornelius coming, and run back to my chair. He's carrying a clear teapot. There's toast and muffins, bowls for soup. The tray is silver, the nap-kins are folded and clean. The spoons are tiny, like doll spoons, and the teacups have letter C handles.

I use my best manners, asking him if he needs help. Setting my napkin on my lap and not slurp-ing the soup. We have the best time until the food is gone and the cat smells are back. I don't want to spoil things. I keep telling Cornelius that I have to get home. Only, he brings out dessert: two glazed doughnuts and vanilla ice cream with sprinkles. He says I must sample them before I go. I am polite. "I am too full."

He hands them to me anyhow.

I am so proud of me: even though the cat smell is making my stomach ache I don't say a word. But a few minutes later, after my food is gone, I get a good idea. "If you cleaned your house you'd have more friends."

Cornelius stares at me like I have snakes on my head. Then he says for me to leave and never come back.

CHAPTER 23

FOR FOUR DAYS I get to stay home with Mother. I tell her I am sick. I itch and scratch and drink milk so I gag, and she lets me stay home. Leroy comes to visit.

"I'm still not talking to you," he says, sitting on the end of my bed. "But I brought you the homework assignments and I wanted to see if you were ever coming back to school."

"What?"

He thanks my mother for the brownies she hands him. He tells me that some kids say I am never coming back because nobody likes me. "I think they will be glad if you stay gone forever."

I ask Leroy if he wants me back. For a long time he doesn't answer. "If your mother was in class, I would like that. If your father was a kid there, I'd like that too. But I don't like you being in class."

He doesn't say it to be mean. He says it because that's how he feels, I guess. Mother hears him. She looks like she wants to cry.

"Can't you be a little nice?" he asks. "Sometimes?"

Mother leaves the room and then comes back in and tells Leroy to let me rest. When he goes home, she says maybe I need help being nice to people. "Trying to do the right thing is hard sometimes."

I hug her. She squeezes me supertight. I tell her that learning new words is easy for me, and doing math problems is a breeze. "But being nice to people is the hardest thing."

Mother is the best mother in the world. She

tells me how much she loves me, how much fun being kind to people is when you get used to it. And all that afternoon she sits on my bed and pretends to be James, Leroy, Markeeta, and Melnick. "I don't like your dress," she says to me.

Sometimes I say the wrong thing. Other times I just say, "Oh. I like your shoes" or "That's okay. I like my dress anyhow. Would you like to play with me?"

Father comes home and gives Mother a big kiss on the lips when she lets him in on what we're doing. For the next three days we practice and practice. I'm scared I will get it all wrong once I'm back at school. But I'm gonna try. I promise them both that I will.

I tell Leroy I'll do better too. He's riding his bike to school. This morning Father said he would drive me, like usual, but I said I'd walk. Leroy rides slowly so I can keep up. He gets off his bike and walks it. "I won't let them be mean to you."

I look at him.

"But you'd better not be mean to them first."

As soon as we get in the school yard, kids start

saying that I'm his girlfriend. I stick the end of my braid in my mouth so I won't talk back. I go over to Jessica and ask her and Markeeta if I can jump rope with them. "No," they both tell me.

I put my braid in my mouth again. Then take it out and say that it's okay that they don't want to play. "Can I watch anyhow?"

Jessica stops turning, and Whitina, the girl jumping, trips on the ropes. She yells at me. Says if I was minding my own business it would not have happened. I can feel mean words bubbling up in me like too much soda up your nose, and right when I'm about to say something horrible, Leroy walks over. "She doesn't want to jump with you anyhow," he says, pulling me away.

But I think about Mother, and I don't go. "It's okay, Leroy. I'll just watch."

Nobody is nice to me today. Nobody wants to be around me. But it isn't so bad, trying to be nice. Like Mother says, the mean in me has to melt away like ice. "That way, people will finally see the nice." Yesterday she said, "It's gonna take time. But it's gonna come. And when it does, you'll have a million friends. Just watch and see."

CHAPTER 24

LEROY ASKS ME to do him a favor. He wants me to go to the store for Cornelius. "It's just up the block."

He can't go because his mother is taking him to the doctor's. I don't want to go because I don't think Cornelius will let me come visit him again. Leroy says I have to do it. "Payback for all the mean you did to me."

I owe him. One girl ate lunch with me the

other day because of him. "I think Leroy is cute," she said. "Can you make him be my boyfriend?"

At the store, I pick up cat food, milk, apples, blueberries, chicken breasts, and a bag of spearmint candy. I knock on Cornelius's door. He opens it, takes the bag, and shuts the door. I don't try to make him let me in. I walk away. That's when the door opens. I apologize right away. Cornelius says he knows that I am sorry. "Because a queen is never rude on purpose."

I sit down on the couch, watching him open cans and calling the cats to eat. They come from everywhere.

Cornelius's house looks different. The boxes are almost gone. The couch is in the same place, but the lopsided, silver Christmas tree isn't around. Something else is different, only I can't figure out what.

I try to be as sweet as pie, even though being so nice to everyone today gave me a headache. Cornelius sits across from me and starts talking.

"Leroy and I went to Africa once."

I look at him to see if he's fibbing.

"We flew in a jet plane and went first class and

it took eighteen hours to get there." He sips coffee. "We stayed in the city, in a nice cool hotel the color of the morning sun." He crosses his legs and feeds red cake crumbs to a green-eyed cat. "We walked to the Sphinx and rode double-humped camels to the Pyramids." We both close our eyes. "And before the sun rose each morning, we swam in the Nile; the water's blue like eyes and warm as a baby's belly."

I . . . I can see it. Feel the warm breeze blowing.

"Queen," he says.

"Yeah?"

"You would love Africa. The colors are so beautiful, so brilliant, they make you want to cry."

I am getting sad.

"And the people, oh my, they hug you for no real reason, and do for you every chance they get." He pats an empty seat next to him. "'Mister, please sit,' they say. 'Eat. Rest. You are our guest.'"

I stare at him. "Did they . . . did they like Leroy, too?"

Cornelius pours Moroccan coffee for me and tells me about their trip. Leroy wore white robes and slippers made of silk. He got carried around the city on a straw mat by four men tall as giraffes.

They gave him gold coins and sand that he poured into bottles. In my imagination, I am with Leroy too—loving everything I see.

"Come," Cornelius says, taking my hand, leading me through the kitchen to a room so wonderful I cannot shut my eyes—not even to blink.

CHAPTER 25

TWO BROWN WOODEN WOMEN with
spears in their hands and orange wraps on their
heads guard the room. Sand, seashells, and stones
cover the floor, so I take off my sneakers and socks
and watch where I step.

Shiny brown stools with elephants carved into
them sit around the room like they are waiting for
people to come take a ride. Women carrying bowls
of fruit on their heads, babies on their hips, and

baskets of clothes on their shoulders walk across the room in magazine pictures glued to the walls.

Masks are everywhere. Some as big as pizza pans, others small as my face. Some masks are covered in beads—red, blue, black—others have long, dry, brown string for hair. There are scary masks, and ones that make you laugh. I touch everything. Cornelius says it's okay.

There is a picture of Cornelius and Leroy. They are standing on a beach with pink sand squished between their toes. I wish I were there with them.

Cornelius takes me to another room. It is filled with books, floor to ceiling. So many books, you have to walk in the room sideways. "You must, you must be the smartest man on earth."

He laughs. "I know some things, yes."

We go back to Africa, and I sit on an elephant named Lucy. Cornelius tells me about his adventures. He asks me questions about my crowns. We talk until my tongue hurts. He leaves the room and comes back with a long piece of cloth. It's bright red with gold threads running through it; the material looks just like Leroy's mother's gown. He sits it across my lap. It's from Zambia. The kind of cloth women make into dresses. "You may keep it, Queen," he says, bowing. "So you will remember your trip to Africa."

I ask a million questions. Like where'd he get all of that gold? Are elephants really as big as they look in the zoo? Did he first meet Leroy in Senegal, and then help his family escape to the States?

He puts his finger to his lips. "Some secrets should stay secret, no?"

I am so excited, so happy, I can burst. My eyes keep going from one wall to another. I stare at the sand and think about the guards at the door. Are they there to protect everything? Did they come here by boat along with Leroy? "Are there real queens in Africa still?" I finally ask Cornelius.

Cornelius nods his head. "A few." He pulls a book from the top of a shelf and blows dust off. He opens the pages slowly, leans down and points to a woman in the picture. "She is a queen from a long, long time ago."

I touch her crown, and my fingers pat her dress.

"She was kind, generous, and strong." His

voice changes. "And I'm telling you, girl-child, she knew how to run a kingdom."

"How? How did she run it?"

He takes my hand and puts it to my heart like I'm going to say the Pledge of Allegiance. "With a kind heart and a great mind."

I stare at her.

"You are like her, you know. Smart."

"I know."

Cornelius winks. He bows and hands me a coin. "All queens are smart. And they all have kind hearts."

"Me too?"

"Especially you."

For a long time he talks about his trips. He tells me how he delivered a hippopotamus's baby and about the time he rode a crocodile to town. "But Africa's not all like that, you know. It's big cities and fast cars too. Just like in this country."

When we are back in the living room, I realize what's different about his place. It smells okay. Not like cat or old things left in the rain. It just smells like a house—anybody's house almost.

I ask him again if Leroy is from Africa. He

speaks French at first. "*Nous tous sommes africains, ma gamine.*" Then he repeats himself in English. "We are all from Africa, child."

It is getting late. I've stayed longer than usual. Through his cracked window I hear Mother calling me. I get up to leave. Cornelius reminds me to take my cloth. He says for me to tell my parents where I got it. To let them know that we are friends and they may come visit him, if they like.

Father would like going to Africa and talking to Cornelius about plays. "I'll tell them. They'll come visit, too."

On the way out, I ask how he can buy food for Leroy if he never leaves his apartment. He bends down to my size. "You always find a way to help people who you love."

"So you leave here sometimes?"

"Maybe." He stands and winks. "I imagine if I could get to the Pyramids, I could get to the store if I really needed to."

I wish Cornelius wasn't so full of riddles. I tell him so, too. And what does he do? He gives me another clue. I listen. He talks. It's almost like his words have legs that walk.

"Read a book
Take a trip
See the stars, or even Mars
Don't want to go that far?
Make a kangaroo or jelly fish your car
Dial a phone
Help a friend
Chicken and burgers fly right in
Stuck inside?
Use your mind
It's a tool that's perfect each
    and every time."

I have it figured out. "Well," I say, "does Leroy
also travel this way?"

Cornelius smiles. "I've seen the world in more
ways than one. Leroy, well, he's had his own kind
of fun."

I ask him about the gold and the elephant tusk.
He gives me another riddle I've got to think through.

"Friends
Stores
Visitors from foreign shores

Treasures are found in more ways than one
So take your pick, and keep having fun."

I hug him good-bye and run down the steps to
tell Mother all about my trip across the world.

CHAPTER 26

"WHAT YOU GOT THERE?"

A boy, and a girl with pink hair pull the cloth from my hand. "You don't live here," the girl says, snatching my book bag too.

They are bigger than me. Teenagers. They don't have a right to take what's mine, so I snatch my things back. The girl doesn't like that. She says that because I'm trying to act so big and bad, she's going to make me pay her money to get outside.

I don't have any money. So I tell her to get out of my way. I accidentally step on her foot. She pushes me. I want to push back, but well, she is bigger than me. "Move," I say. "Please."

The boy laughs. He says I have a lot of guts for a little kid. The girl doesn't like that. She takes the cloth and drops it and steps on it with her dirty shoes. I pick it up and brush it off. She digs in my pockets, dumps out my backpack, and goes through my wallet. I only have ten cents, which is not enough for her. "You not leaving till you pay up. So you'd better find some money from someplace."

She shoves me out the door. I look up to see if Mother is staring out the window. She's not. The boy says it's stupid to rob a kid with no cash, and he leaves. The girl says she's gonna teach me a lesson. I try to bite her finger, but it doesn't stop her. And just when she is about to hit me, Leroy comes by riding that broken bike. It doesn't have a seat. It doesn't have a silver horn, and it isn't even blue anymore.

He rides circles around me and the girl.

She grabs me, knocks the cloth to the ground, and laughs.

Leroy jumps off his bike while it's still moving. "Get off her now, before I hurt you!" The bike runs into the bushes and the wheels spin.

She laughs, turns me loose, and goes after Leroy, swinging her fists and almost catching him.

I'm staring at her, because now I remember. She took the money from the blind man. I wait till she gets closer to the bike. "You ugly, stupid thing!" I say, pointing to the pink hair sticking out of her head like scaly spikes.

Girls don't like being called names. So she stops. Fire comes out of her nose, and her long arms swing out like a dragon's tail, just about knocking Leroy down. That makes Leroy angry. And right then he pushes her over the bike and into the bushes. "Run," he says, taking my hand.

When we're almost across the street I stop and yell, "My sneaker!" It had come off my foot. "My gown! Cornelius gave it to me."

Cars rush by, just missing my beautiful sneaker. Leroy turns around, bouncing on his toes, ready to run back for my things. I hold on to his arm because I can see the girl pulling herself out of the bushes and brushing off her clothes. I want Leroy to be safe. But I want what belongs to me too. After a few minutes of trying to think what to do, I tell him not to bother. "I can always get more things."

Leroy doesn't listen to me. He flies across the street, snatching up my sneaker and ducking busses and cars. The girl swings a stick at him. He drops low to the ground, and jumps up quick—like he knows karate. The dragon-girl throws a punch; then a kick. Leroy does too, only you can tell he doesn't know exactly what he's doing. So he gives her a good, hard shove and down she goes, tripping over the bike again.

For a little while, he just stares at her, like maybe he's thinking he should help her up. Then he picks up my cloth, and runs to me with the street-light shining on him like a giant moon. He hands me my new purple sneaker, the one with the satin laces, silver stars, and golden crowns painted on it. We sit on the curb, watching the girl ride away with his bike. Leroy tells me before I ask that he gave his real bike to a boy who didn't have one. I am thinking about all of my father's hard work. That's when Leroy says that he likes old bikes' seats better, anyhow. "They make you go faster. Besides, people always throw bikes in the trash, so I can get another one tomorrow."

I don't get mad. I think about Father. He will be glad to help Leroy fix up another bike. I think about Mother, and how proud she will be that I didn't get mad at Leroy for doing something stupid with his first bike. And I think about Symone and how I will tell her everything when I write her tomorrow. "We will always be friends," I wrote in my last letter to her.

Mother opens the window and calls my name. We laugh, because we know she can't see us sitting down on the curb. Leroy whispers, "Did you go into Cornelius's place? Did he let you ride Lucy?"

I put on my sneaker. He ties it. I look at the moon, and the stars that match my beautiful sneaker stars perfectly. "I rode Lucy and saw all his books and the masks and . . ."

"Queen Marie Rosseau." Mother's voice is louder now. "It's dark. And I want you in this house right now."

I tell her we are just right out front. She wants me inside anyhow. "Leroy. We're having coconut fried shrimp, curried rice, and peas. Queen's favorites. Bet you'd like them too."

Leroy rubs his stomach and licks his lips. We both look back across the street where the dragon-girl was. "I get to take home extras, right?"

Of course Mother says yes.

I hadn't thought about it, but I am starving. Fighting dragons and walking across Africa make you hungry. "Let's go eat," I say, standing up.

Leroy carries my cloth and opens the door to our apartment building. "I'm going to eat everything in your whole house—maybe even the couch."

I laugh. The moon shines. And then he and I run up to my balcony holding hands and talking about bad girls, elephants, and Africa.

Cornelius gave Queen a tough riddle to figure out. If you were able to follow all of the clues and come up with the correct answers, then you must be one smart cookie; just like Queen. So congratulations on using your noodle. If you didn't figure out the country and other interesting tidbits that Cornelius's riddle pointed to, don't worry. We've provided you with the answers right here. Have fun.

The clues in the riddle all point to a country in Africa called Liberia. Liberia, which means "Land of the Free," lies on the North Atlantic Ocean in the southern part of West Africa. Its neighbors are Sierra Leone, Guinea, and Côte d'Ivoire. Liberia, Africa's first republic, was founded by free-born and formerly enslaved blacks from America. Approximately 15,000 freed slaves were relocated to the country over a forty-year period. In 2005, Liberians elected Africa's first female head of state, Ellen Johnson-Sirleaf.

Liberia has fifteen counties, one of which is Maryland, named after the state of Maryland in America. Former American slaves, who relocated in Liberia, often named their new settlements after states they were previously residents of, including Louisiana and Mississippi.

West Africa has a rich cultural history. It is also home to some of the world's most magnificent beaches, floral life, and animals, including the Diana monkey. The Diana monkey is an endangered species. It can be found in the tropical rain forests of Liberia, Ghana, Guinea, Côte d'Ivoire, Zaire, and Sierra Leone. Diana monkeys live in groups of fifteen to fifty, with only one male among them. Daughters stay with their mothers for life, while males leave their birth group upon adolescence. The Diana monkey usually has a black head, white beard, chest, and throat, a stripe down each thigh, and a reddish-brown patch on its back.

3 1192 01494 1312